Co
St

Nancy Gorrell

CHRISTIAN FOCUS

ISBN 13 978-1-84550-258-4
Published in 2007 by
Christian Focus Publications,
Geanies House, Fearn, Tain
Ross-shire, IV20 1TW,
Great Britain
Cover design by Danie van Straaten
Cover illustration and inside illustrations
by Kim Sponaugle
Printed and Bound in Denmark
by Nørhaven Paperback A/S

Contents

Who is Corey?

Corey Redmond is an American boy a lot like many other American boys, and maybe a little like you! He and his mom are new at their church. Sometimes his dad comes too, but not often—not yet anyway.

Corey is learning about God and about God's Son, the Savior, the Lord Jesus. He is learning to love God, but that doesn't mean he's perfect!

Sometimes Corey has to work hard at being good. Sometimes his old friends still want him to get into trouble. Corey is discovering that God's Word and God's Spirit are the help he always needs.

Corey loves to play soccer. He's pretty good at it too! Oh, it looks like the Panthers are in the middle of a game. Let's join them...

Goal!

It was almost up. Time was almost up, but there it was. The goal! Corey was so very close, and he had the ball.

Everything was a blur, except for the gigantic goalie in front of him. Almost without thinking, Corey felt his foot connect with the ball, the way he had practiced so many times. And, for the first time, the ball did exactly what he wanted it to do—it flew right past those incredibly long goalie arms, right into the corner. Right into the net!

Yells of triumph came from Corey's teammates. Time was up! They won! They won! It was their first victory.

Corey was in a big jumble of hopping, shouting boys. "Hooray! Hooray!" "Way to go, Corey!" "We won! We won!" "The Panthers are the best!"

He saw his friend Anna in the bleachers squealing with excitement. "Yay, Corey! Yay, hooray, Corey!" He gave her the thumbs up.

There was a big grin and a pat on the back

from Coach Williams. "Nice work, Corey!"

There was a high five and "Great shot, Son!" from dad.

There was a proud hug from mom. It was the perfect moment.

On the ride home Corey was tired, but the victory left him warm and tingly all the way to his toes. He dreamed about his next great shot.

Later that afternoon his friend and teammate Marcus was at the door. He gave Corey an

enthusiastic punch and did a victory dance. "Way to go, buddy! I can't believe we won!"

They sat on the steps and talked about the game until there was hardly anything left to say.

"Let's practice," Marcus said.

"Sure!" Corey agreed. "Maybe I can teach you some of my great moves."

They ran and kicked and ran and kicked and sweated, and Corey demonstrated the Victory Shot so many times that Marcus began to grow a little tired of it. "You be goalie now, Corey. Let me try a few." But Corey ignored him, and Marcus finally decided that it was time to go home.

"Where's Marcus?" Mrs. Redmond asked as Corey sat down in the kitchen.

"Oh, he had to go home," Corey responded. "Besides, I think he was a little jealous."

"Why would you think that?" his mom said.

"Well, he just didn't seem to want to let me

practice my winning shots."

"Oh...well, Corey, did you let him try some too?"

"Yeah, I did, but Marcus just doesn't have as many great moves as I do," Corey answered as he put down his empty glass and left the kitchen.

The news of Corey's winning goal had reached Sunday School ahead of him. Anna had happily told the teacher before he arrived. "Congratulations, Corey!" Mrs. Wheeler said as he entered the room. Corey couldn't stop smiling.

At prayer time, Mrs. Wheeler praised the Lord for His blessings to the children in the class. She thanked God for helping Corey to play well and for giving Corey's team a victory. I'll bet my buddies are thankful I'm on their team! thought Corey. And he daydreamed through most of Sunday School.

Corey arrived triumphantly at the next practice session. He found his teammates in the midst of an excited buzz. But the buzz was not about him, and the center of attention was Coach Williams - Coach, and a very large, healthy-looking, athletic boy who happened to be standing next to him.

"Who is he?" he asked Marcus.

"I don't know—he looks too old to be on our team."

"Wouldn't it be great if he were going to play with us? He's huge!" another boy said.

Coach was smiling as he walked toward the whispering group. "Hello, boys!"

"Hi, Coach!" was the excited reply.

"Listen, team, I'd like you to meet Evan."

Everyone was silent.

"He's going to be our new player." Some cheers went up, but Coach quieted them. "I know he's missed two games, but he has just come to stay with his aunt who lives nearby, while his folks are traveling. He'll play for the rest of the season and

will be a great addition to the team! So, let's give Evan a big welcome to the Panthers!"

Corey watched jealously as the Hero's Greeting he had expected was given to this over-sized stranger. He even saw Marcus join in enthusiastically. "What's the big deal?" he thought. "I won the last game. He hasn't even played a single time with us. He can't be that good."

But Evan was big and he was fast and he was very good, as they all learned that afternoon.

Corey liked Evan less and less as Evan kicked goal after goal around him and his teammates.

"I'm as good as he is—I'll show him." But practice was over, and Corey didn't even have one satisfying opportunity to show off. Nobody seemed to care anymore that Corey was the one with the Victory Shot that had won their last game.

The next game day came. The excitement was high. With Evan on the team, Corey's teammates thought, victory was certain.

But it was a hard game, a long and difficult game, and nothing happened for either team. The game was almost over; everyone was sweaty and worried, and the score was stuck at 0 – 0.

Coach tried to encourage the saggy boys. "All right, Panthers, you're doing a good job. You're working hard, and I'm proud of you. We have the ball now, so let's try one last thing and see how it goes. Let's see if we can get our new teammate Evan in good position and send him the ball."

"Evan!" Corey thought. "I won the last game. What's so great about him?"

As the boys struggled to get the ball in place for a shot, Corey found himself with it. He looked up to see Evan's waving arms. Evan had a clear view of the goal. Corey didn't. But Corey wanted to be the hero. So Corey kicked with all his might and waited for the cheers. They came, but they were from the other team as the ball soared out-of-bounds.

The game ended as it began, 0 – 0. Corey didn't have a warm, tingly feeling on this ride home. He was upset and grumpy and embarrassed. Oh, how he wished he had scored that goal and won the game! His parents attempted to cheer him, but he didn't tell them the real reason he felt so terrible.

Anna smiled kindly at Corey as he arrived in church the next day. "I'm sorry you lost, Corey."

"It's OK," Corey shrugged carelessly and put on a fake smile. "Besides, we didn't lose; we tied, and that's not so bad."

All of a sudden, the room got strangely quiet. Everyone was looking at the door. Mrs. Wheeler smiled at the two figures standing there. "Oh, good, Evan, I've been expecting you!"

Evan! Corey stared. Evan! Not him! And who is that with him? Corey wondered. It was sweet Miss Hawkins, who always so bright and pretty. *That* Miss Hawkins is Evan's aunt! Oh, bother. Thought Corey.

Evan actually looked a little shy, standing in the doorway. He saw Corey and his face lit up. Someone he knew! He came and sat next to Corey, and Corey pretended to be happy to see him.

Mrs. Wheeler started cheerfully. "Have you all enjoyed the stories from the book of Daniel?"

"Yes!" was the reply from the children.

"Today," said Mrs. Wheeler, "we study a very strange thing that happened to King Nebuchadnezzar and taught him that God is the one who is the real King and that He is the one who gives us every good thing that we enjoy. God is the one whom we should praise and thank whenever we are blessed."

Mrs. Wheeler then told the remarkable story of King Nebuchadnezzar from Daniel chapter 4. This ruler thought that his excellent kingdom was all his own doing. His heart was proud and haughty. But God showed the king that He was the one who gave men ability and strength. God made the king no better than an animal! He ate grass like an ox and grew fingernails like bird claws. Then, just as easily, God gave him back his right mind and his throne. Nebuchadnezzar learned an important lesson. He finally understood that God was the true King and that pride was wrong. God was the one who had given him a great kingdom, and God should be thanked and served in it.

Corey listened to the tale with astonishment and then with shame. He felt like the lesson was taught just for him! How proud he had been. He had never even thanked God for his winning shot. Then he had spent all his energy at soccer trying to show everyone that he was better than Evan. He was so busy being jealous and proud that he hadn't even thought about being Evan's friend. He looked guiltily at the smiling boy sitting next to him. And besides all that, his pride had hurt his whole team yesterday! It had lost them the game.

"Forgive me, God," his heart whispered, "for being so proud. Help me to do better. Thank you for my new friend. Oh, and thanks for giving me a great goal the other day too!"

Later, Corey gladly invited Evan to sit with his family during church, while Miss Hawkins sang in the choir.

The next practice went beautifully. Corey worked hard with his team and didn't try to show off once. Coach Williams noticed his attitude and praised him after practice was over. Corey smiled and said thanks to God. He even caught up with Marcus before he left and apologized for being so selfish the week before.

Finally, the day for game four arrived—the Panthers and Mustangs eyed each other from across the field. Everyone was ready to play!

And what a game it was! Evan was in excellent form. Corey admired his teammate's skill as Evan scored two sizzling goals. The other team had its heroes too, however; and, despite their effort, the Panthers found themselves behind, 3 – 2. The boys hoped that Evan would pull them ahead again, but he just didn't have the opportunity.

Finally, Corey saw Evan with the ball and a clear shot. As several Mustangs rushed over to prevent his scoring, Corey was alone. Now Evan was no longer free, but somehow, miraculously—it seemed to Corey—Evan was able to pass the ball over to him.

Corey looked nervously at the goal. He could hear Evan shouting to him, "Do it, Corey, do it!" So with a deep breath, and a prayer, Corey gave the ball a mighty kick. 'Please!' he thought, 'let it go in! Oh no!' Corey's heart sank. 'Too wide.'

Yet, suddenly, there was Evan's curly head, right

in the path of the ball. And, to the amazement of the spectators, that dark forehead gave the ball the little correction that it needed. It was a gentle tap, past the astonished goalie, right into the net! Corey had never seen a kid his age do that before! Evan had scored again!

Of course, everyone erupted in cheers, and even the other team was impressed. The Panthers' spirits soared, and they truly put their energy and hearts into the rest of the game. Nevertheless, not even Evan's heroic head could win the victory that

day. Still, all agreed that the very best part of the contest had been that terrific goal. Both teams went home, satisfied with a well-fought 3 – 3 tie.

Corey and Evan were drinking lemonade in the Redmond's kitchen that afternoon while talking about the events of the day.

"Evan," Corey said humbly, "can you teach me to use my head like that?"

"Sure," Evan replied cheerfully, and butted foreheads with him. "It definitely seems hard enough!"

ASK ABOUT IT

How did Corey feel about scoring the winning goal?

How should Corey have felt about it?

What Bible story helped Corey to realize his sinful attitude?

With God's help, what changes did Corey make?

Whom should you thank for your blessings and talents?

LESSON SPOT

Corey loved to play soccer, and he wanted very much to be good at it. When he finally scored a winning goal, he was thrilled. And that's not wrong! God is pleased when we enjoy and use the gifts He's given us. The important thing to remember is that our Lord is the One who has blessed us with our talents. We honor Him when we use our skills thankfully and to His glory. When we take selfish pride in the gifts and ignore the Giver, it dishonors our God. Your blessings, Christian children, are a token of His love. They should always make you thankful and point you to God's greatest gift—our Savior the Lord Jesus!

ASK YOURSELF

If you won a race at a sporting event but your brother didn't, what would you do? Pick your answers.

1. Jump up and down and wave all your prizes in his face.

2. Tell your brother not to waste time at sports. It's obvious he's no use.

3. Tell your brother to take one of your prizes, because he will probably never get a prize and you've got plenty.

4. Praise your brother for something he does well.

5. Ask your brother if he would like you to help him train for the next sports day.

6. Tell everyone how thankful you are that God has given you health and strength.

BIBLE VERSE

1 Corinthians 10:31

So whether you eat or drink
or whatever you do, do it all
for the glory of God.

Go For It!

Corey's mittened hand burned as if he held a rock of fire. He opened his grip to see only the small puff of snow he had formed into a crumbly ball. Loud whispers urged him.

"Go for it, Corey! Throw it! Hurry!"

"Ha! I got her!"

"Rats! I just missed her silly hat!"

The little old lady who was the target for these attacks turned to see the cold-hearted youngsters

across the street. She had a look that was not quite sad, nor was it angry. It stopped the boys for a moment, but they were too proud to be ashamed.

"Come on, Corey! We've only hit her once! What can she do, she's just an old granny!"

The crumbles of snow fell out of Corey's fist onto the sidewalk, and his head hung down.

"What's happened to you, Corey? Been going to Sunday School too long?"

"That's it! Corey's just a Sunday School sissy!"

Corey's schoolmates laughed at him now. Marcus, the group's leader, said, "Corey can stay here and read his Bible!"

A leftover snowball took Corey's hat off as the others galloped away to some different mischief.

So Corey wandered home alone. The icy wind could not cool his flaming cheeks; even his insides were hot, and he felt sad and sorry.

Sunday morning followed a droopy Saturday night. At church he pretended to be cheerful and went to Sunday School again! He waved at his friend Anna Freeling before taking a seat alone in the corner. Anna watched him pass with a puzzled frown. Anna's dad, Pastor Freeling, was teaching their class this week. Corey vaguely remembered that Mrs. Wheeler was out, having a baby or something. The morning's lesson was on Joshua. Corey's mind was elsewhere, but slowly Mr. Freeling's words began to draw pictures in his imagination, and he found himself paying attention.

Very soon Corey was soon wishing that he were a brave warrior for God like Joshua. He had been a coward on Saturday. Four boys had almost tempted him to hurt an old lady! He didn't even have the guts to tell them they were stupid and mean. He was afraid to say anything because he didn't want to lose his friends. Life would be so much easier if he could have lived in Joshua's day. Then God would appear to him and talk to him and would make him brave. Then it would be easy to stand up to the bad guys—he would fight with the enemies of God and win!

"Now, children," Pastor was continuing, "I have chosen some memory verses for you. We are going to find out the real reason that Joshua was such a great warrior for God. Listen carefully while I read Joshua 1, verses 7 through 9:

Only be strong and very courageous, that you may observe to do according to all the law which Moses My servant commanded you; do not turn from it to the right hand or to the left, that you may prosper wherever you go. This Book of the Law shall not depart from your mouth, but you shall meditate in it day and night, that you may observe to do

according to all that is written in it. For then you will make your way prosperous, and then you will have good success. Have I not commanded you? Be strong and of good courage; do not be afraid, nor be dismayed, for the LORD your God is with you wherever you go.

"God made Joshua a mighty warrior, but what important thing did God tell Joshua to do first?"

Anna's eyes were bright. "Joshua was told to be strong and brave to obey God's commandments!"

"Is it hard to do what is right sometimes?"

"Oh, yes," was the general chorus.

"But you are to be brave to obey! Listen once more, children. What will make us strong and courageous to obey?"

Pastor Freeling read the verses again. Corey felt his face grow warm as the words seemed to come right out of his Bible and swell up in his heart. "You can be brave to do what is right because God will always be with you," he said hoarsely, more to himself than to his teacher.

Pastor smiled kindly at him and patted his

shoulder. "You're exactly right, Corey. God is the only one who can make us brave, and He is always with us, ready and happy to help us to do what is right."

Corey marked his Bible carefully. He didn't think the verses would be so hard to remember, as the words seemed to be burned onto his brain.

Be strong and of good courage, do not be afraid, nor be dismayed, for the Lord your God is with you wherever you go.

Corey felt a little queasy on Monday morning. He was tempted to lie, so that he could stay home, but he did what was right and got ready to see his classmates. God was with him.

As he walked up the steps to the school building, Marcus teasingly punched his arm, "Hey sissy-boy!" But Marcus actually seemed pretty friendly. Corey was relieved.

The other boys soon arrived and gathered in a cluster on the steps. "Hey, Corey!" "Hi, Core!" and so on. No one said any more about the other afternoon. Neither did Corey.

Another car pulled up to the curb, and Tony Reynolds climbed out. Tony was a year older than Corey and his friends. He was a big, bold boy who could get away with all sorts of daring misdeeds. The younger lads were in awe of him, as well as a little fearful. They felt honored when he noticed them this morning with a "Hi ya, fellows!"

He shut the car door. "Later, Granny!" he grunted and turned toward the group. It was only then that the boys on the step noticed the car's driver.

The elderly woman behind the wheel looked very familiar. All hearts sank. Oh, doom! Saturday's snowball target was Tony Reynolds' grandmother! She smiled kindly at them before driving away.

Tony appeared to block the whole staircase as he lazily climbed toward the clustered boys. "What's up, guys?" he cheerily asked. Could it be that Mrs. Reynolds hadn't told him of what they'd done?

Yes. Little Mrs. Reynolds had mysteriously chosen to keep their unkind deeds a secret from her grandson. One by one, they stopped fidgeting and began to take some pride in his attention. Corey found himself laughing along with the other fellows. He forgot all about the Sunday School lesson, and anyway, they really weren't doing anything bad right now. Besides, Tony was cool, and everyone at school knew it.

At noon, the cafeteria clattered with voices and silverware. Corey found a seat and was soon joined by Marcus and the three other boys.

"Wow! Can you believe it? Tony Reynolds hung out with us this morning!"

Across the lunch hall, Tony was among his regular friends. Their heads were together as they formulated some grand plot. Then, to the wonder of Corey and his young pals, Tony made his way over to them! "Hey guys! What's up?"

This was great. Tony Reynolds was actually sitting down with them.

"Hi, Tony! Not much," Marcus was able to reply. "What's up with you?"

Tony's eyebrows went up, and his smile was sneaky. "I've got a great plan. But I need your help."

'Our help?' The boys all wondered.

"Great!" as self-appointed leader, Marcus spoke for everyone. "Tell us what to do."

Tony grinned, very pleased with this answer. "I hear you guys will do just about anything. In fact, my pal Joe said he saw you throwing snowballs at an old lady the other day!" He laughed appreciatively. Joe sneered at them and winked. Corey, Marcus and the others then realized that Joe knew everything! If they didn't join in with Tony and his gang then Joe would spill the beans and Tony would beat them to a pulp!

Corey gulped as Tony enthusiastically explained what he wanted. "We have a killer math test coming up next Friday. If we don't pass it, we'll have to waste half the summer in stupid, boring summer school!" he rolled his eyes. "Some of the fourth graders told us that Mr. Horst does his tests a week ahead, so he can get them typed into the computer. Now, here's the good part," Tony grinned. "We think that one of you boys should get that test for us. You're young enough to sneak it out of his room without raising any suspicion. When he's at lunch you could get into

the classroom, copy it, and put it back. He'll never know. My friends and I will pass the test, and you guys get instant cool! What do you think?"

Four sets of eyes sparkled with the challenge. Strategies were already being developed. Corey felt sick. Stealing and cheating. This was getting really bad.

He looked up to see Marcus staring at him, eyebrows down. "Tony, you have come to the right place. We can plan this, easy. I think that Corey is definitely the man for the job."

"Excellent!" Tony admired Corey with a satisfied nod. "Corey's the man! Thanks, guys. See you later!" and he was off.

Corey was nearly feverish that afternoon. Things were getting really, really bad. Once school was out, he set his face straight for the door and spoke to no one. He made it outside, breathed relief, and started walking home, when a sharp pull on his arm halted him. He spun around to face Marcus!

"Not so fast, Sunday School boy," he growled. "Don't you dare spoil this one, Corey. If you rat on us, you'll get your face punched, and the whole school will know that you're a wimpy little church boy!"

Corey's heart beat hard. "I wasn't going to rat on you." He yanked his arm away. "And why don't you steal the test? Are you afraid to do it?"

"No way. You're the sissy, remember? I just want to know whether your Bible stories are going to ruin our fun or get us into trouble. Face it, Corey, you're in this now. If you don't get that test, Joe is going to tell Tony that you were the one throwing snowballs last Saturday and that the old lady you hit was Tony's granny! Tony will squash you like a bug! Don't mess with this, Corey!"

Corey felt awful. Things were looking really, really, really bad. He wanted to sit down somewhere and cry, but he couldn't do that, not in public anyway. Now his verses were roaring in his head, reminding him that he was a coward and that being a coward had gotten him into a huge mess. Corey then realized that it wasn't really the verses that he had ignored. He had forgotten Jesus. He hadn't been brave to obey his Savior.

What was he going to do? He couldn't steal that test. Even if Tony punched his face so hard that it turned inside outward, he couldn't do it.

All of a sudden Corey was ringing a doorbell. A door opened, and Anna was there, smiling at him. "Hi, Corey! Corey, what's the matter?"

"A—a—anna," he stammered, finally thinking about what he was actually doing. "Uh, I mean, uh, well, is your dad home, I mean, can he talk to me maybe?"

"Hi, Corey," the voice was above his head, and he looked up to see Pastor Freeling's puzzled smile. "I'd love to talk to you. Please come in."

Corey could hardly look Pastor Freeling in the eye. As they settled themselves down the Pastor asked, "Corey, is there something that I can help you with?"He sounded like he really did want to help.

"Yes—well—maybe–well, I hope so."

"What is it, Corey?"

Corey took a deep breath and looked at Pastor Freeling. Seeing his kind eyes, he felt braver and forced himself to start. "What if you did something sort of bad, but it could have been worse, but it was bad enough because you were afraid to do what was really right; and then because of it and because of being afraid, you got into a worse situation, and all of a sudden someone wants you to do something very bad? And you know you can't do it, but you're afraid to and afraid not to?"

Pastor put his hand on his chin and looked carefully at Corey as he followed the tumble of words. "Well, Corey, that sounds serious. I have several questions to ask you about it."

Corey sat up straighter.

"First, have you talked to your parents about this problem?"

"No, sir," Corey was ashamed to admit.

"Why not?"

"Because if I tattle, I'll get my face punched."

"OK. I can understand your fear. But your parents might be able to help you without you getting your face punched. God gave them to you for a reason—to love, protect, and guide you."

"Yes, sir."

"Next, the thing that you did that was wrong. Have you repented for it?"

"Repented?"

"Are you sad for it, have you asked God to forgive you, and are you determined not to behave that way again?"

"Well, maybe. I'm sure going to try not to behave that way again!"

"Have you asked the person that you hurt, if you did hurt someone, to forgive you?"

"No."

"Then you need to do that. The Bible says you are to go to the one you have sinned against and ask his or her forgiveness."

"Yes, sir."

"Here's my last question, Corey. The 'bad thing' that you talked about, has it been done yet?"

"No, sir."

"Is it possible for you to go to every other person who knows about this, one at a time, and tell them that you cannot do it? Explain to them why and encourage them to stop it too. Then you not only help yourself but them as well."

"I guess I could."

"Are you afraid to obey, Corey?"

"Yes," it was only a whisper, almost tearful.

"But you want to do what's right?"

"I really do," Corey's voice squeaked.

"What can make us brave and courageous, Corey?"

"Remembering that God is with me, and that He will help me to succeed if I obey His word."

Pastor smiled. "I guess you did pay attention on Sunday, although it did seem like your head was in a cloud."

"In a snowball, sir."

"What?"

"Never mind."

Mr. Freeling patted Corey's shoulder. "Corey, let's pray together, shall we?"

So they prayed, and Corey's heart talked to his Savior, and he knew that he was forgiven. And, he knew that God would be with him. Still... "Does this mean that I won't get my face punched?"

Pastor laughed. "Corey, sometimes we get our faces punched in this world, especially if we do what's right. Jesus said (not in these exact words, of course) that a black eye can be a mark of honor for a Christian. You are blessed if you are ill-used for His sake."

"OK, but I hope I don't get a black eye."

"I hope so too, Corey. I'll pray about that. Now get going home to your mom. I'll bet she's worried. I'll let her know you're on your way."

"Thanks, Pastor Freeling."

"You're very welcome, Corey."

"Oh, and Pastor, would you tell her that I need her help, but that I really don't want to tattle?"

"Sure, Corey."

There were milk, cookies, and a warm hug waiting for Corey when he got home. "What do we need to do, Corey?"

"Can you drive me to Mrs. Reynolds' house? Do you know Mrs. Reynolds? She's old and...".

"Oh, do you mean the little widow, Mrs.

Reynolds, that goes to church with us? I think she has a grandson in your school, Tony or Tommy, or something like that. He lives with her but spends the weekends with his father."

"She goes to church with us?"

"Yes, dear. I know exactly whom you're talking about. I'll take you right over."

Corey was ringing another doorbell. This time Tony was at the door, looking at him with a puzzled expression. "Hey, Corey! What's up? Do we need to go for a walk, or something?" He looked over his shoulder at his grandmother who was approaching the door.

"No, Tony. I need to talk to your grandmother."

"Oh, really?" Tony's eyes flashed angrily. "What about? I think maybe you just need to go on home, don't you?" His fists were clenched and his face was menacing. He kept his back to his grandmother so that she couldn't see his lips move. "I'll get you, you dirty rat!"

"Well, hello, young man," a pleasant voice was saying. "How can I help you? You're the

Redmond's boy, aren't you?"

Corey's face was hot. She had known him all along. "Yes, ma'am."

"Well, why don't you come in?"

"Granny," Tony looked very tall and very upset. "He doesn't want to come in, now do you, Corey?"

Corey swallowed hard. "Yes, I do." It was just loud enough for Mrs. Reynolds to hear.

"Well, then, fine, come on in. Tony, for the pete's sake, move out of the way and let your friend in the door!"

"He isn't my friend!"

"Tony, please!" She pushed him gently out of the way, to allow Corey to enter. As she moved into a small, neat room, Corey followed her, and Tony was close on his heels.

"Have a seat, dear." Mrs. Reynolds took her place in a rocker and motioned Corey to a faded couch. Tony sat down next to him with his foot uncomfortably on Corey's heel and his elbow sharply in his side. "Now what do we need to talk about?" Her kind face told Corey that she already knew why he was there.

"I just wanted to come over and tell you how sorry I am for what happened the other day. I'm sorry that I even thought about being so mean to you. I'm really sorry that I was a coward and that I didn't help you. It was just terrible to treat someone's grandmother that way. It was terrible." Corey couldn't see her through his blurred eyes. He really looked like a sissy now, but so be it. "Can you ever forgive me?" His voice, his whole body, actually, felt very small and weak and sorry.

There was a thin, but comforting arm around his shoulders, and Corey realized that Tony had been moved to one side and that Mrs. Reynolds was beside him. "Of course, dear boy, of course, I forgive you. Thank you for coming over to speak to me like this. It took courage to do that. Of course, I forgive you." She patted his cheek and squeezed his hand. "You are a dear boy, and

I believe that in the future, you will be a great champion for those who are weak."

"Granny, now wait a minute. Just what is he talking about? What is it? I want you to tell me!"

"Tony, Corey and I have dealt with this, and you need not be concerned with it."

"Granny ...!"

"Tony, that's enough." She sounded quite tough for such a little old lady.

"Now, would you boys like to play some ball together or come into the kitchen for a snack?" Mrs. Reynolds sounded as if Corey were there every day after school.

"No, but thanks very much, Mrs. Reynolds."

Corey got ready for round two. "My mom's waiting, but can I talk to you for just a few minutes, Tony? We can go out back, if you want."

It was Mrs. Reynolds' turn to look puzzled. "Of course, boys, go along then. I'll be right here."

Tony led Corey out a narrow door into an orderly but cramped back yard. "What's up, Corey?" but his voice wasn't menacing, it was flat. He didn't look nearly so tall as he had at the front door.

"Tony, I can't get that test for you. Punch me in the face if you want, but I can't do it. It would be stealing; it would be wrong." Corey was expecting pain, but pain didn't come, so he just kept talking. Tony would probably hit him after school tomorrow; he might as well get it all said now. "You really don't have to cheat, you know. I'm sure Mr. Horst would help you get ready for the test, so that you could pass. Don't you think you could try that instead? Or maybe my mom or your granny could help you study..."

"Corey, it's OK. Forget it."

"What?"

"I said, never mind."

"Really?" It was a bold thing to ask, but he did it anyway—"Are you going to pound me at school tomorrow?"

"No."

"Really?"

"Really!" Tony growled.

"OK," Corey said rather meekly. "But Tony, please don't steal the test! Please don't get those other boys to do it!"

"I'll think about it. Now leave me alone and go home, alright?"

"Yes, Tony." He left Tony sitting on the back porch with his head down. Mrs. Reynolds was rocking, quietly watching her grandson through the window.

"Good-bye, Mrs. Reynolds," Corey called out.

"Good-bye, dear," she said, smiling gently.

His mom looked anxious as Corey climbed into the car. "How did it go? Is everything OK?"

"I think so, Mom. Except..." Now the tears really did flow. "I'm sorry, Mom. I'm sorry."

"Corey, I love you."

"I love you too, Mom."

The following morning it was another school day. He had to face everyone all over again. But this time, he hoped he was ready.

Marcus met him at the front door of the building and eyed him suspiciously. "What's going on, Corey?"

"Oh, not much."

"Rat on us?"

"No."

"Better not have."

Tony's grandmother drove up to the school again. To Marcus' surprise, she waved brightly to Corey as Tony hopped out of the car. "Good morning, Corey!"

"Good morning, Mrs. Reynolds!"

"Corey," growled Marcus, "what did you do?"

Corey felt trapped between Marcus and Tony. Mrs. Reynolds was gone, and that old fear was rising in his throat. He fought it down. Be strong and courageous, for the Lord your God is...

"Corey! What did you do?" Marcus repeated angrily.

"Nothing." It was Tony's voice.

"Oh, yeah?" Marcus sounded doubtful.

"Well, he did stop by the house last night."

"Stopped by the house?"

"Yeah, stopped by the house," Tony nodded. "And, well, my man Corey here convinced me that I am smart enough to pass that test without cheating. I'm not stupid, you know," he looked across at Marcus.

"I didn't say you were, Tony."

"Good. Anyway, I'm not stupid, so I guess I don't need you fellows to get that test for me after all."

"Really?"

"Really." The group had swollen to include all

of Tony's followers and the rest of the boys from Corey's group. They were listening with great interest.

Joe was the only one who looked really mad. Maybe Tony didn't want the test, but he didn't want to have to study if he didn't have to. He still thought that he might be able to scare Corey into getting that test. "Hey, Tony," he laughed, "did I tell you about that little old lady Corey threw the snowball at? You might be interested..."

Tony turned to his friend with a steely gaze, "You know what, Joe, I don't care about what Corey does in his spare time, because Corey and my granny are old friends." Then he added, "I

may not be the sweetest fellow around, but I watch out for my gran and her friends. So, Corey and I have an understanding. Is that clear?"

"Sure, Tony," said Joe, puzzled.

"Great. Now you guys go on. I need to talk to Corey here in private."

Everyone disappeared quickly.

"Corey, are you all right?" Tony was now laughing at him. "You look really white!" and he gave Corey a friendly punch in the arm.

Corey laughed back, with relief and happiness. "I'm fine, Tony. I'm just great!"

ASK ABOUT IT

What did Corey's friends want him to do?

Was it hard for Corey to stand up to his friends and to do what was right?

Have your friends ever asked you to do something wrong?

How did godly grown-ups help Corey?

What Bible verses helped Corey to be brave?

LESSON SPOT

Corey had friends who didn't love Jesus, and they tried to talk Corey into being unkind, stealing, and cheating. Although Corey had become a Christian and he knew these sins were bad, it was hard for him to say no. He forgot that God was with him, even in difficult situations, so his friends seemed bigger than his God. Remember to choose friends wisely. It is better to have godly friends who help you to be good, than ungodly friends who tempt you to be naughty. Most importantly, though, remember that Jesus is your greatest and only perfect friend. Walk with Him every day, talk to Him, trust Him, and learn His word. Be strong and courageous, for the Lord your God is with you wherever you go.

ASK YOURSELF

What should you do when friends ask you to do something that you know is wrong? Pick your answers.

1. Go along with it. Nobody will know.

2. Tell them that they can go ahead but you'll just watch.

3. Leave them to get on with it. But tell them that you won't say anything.

4. Tell them that what they are doing is wrong and against God.

5. Go straight home and tell a grown-up about what has happened.

6. Pray with that grown-up that God will show you what to do in the future.

BIBLE VERSE

Joshua 1:9

Have I not commanded you? Be strong and courageous. Do not be terrified; do not be discouraged, for the LORD your God will be with you wherever you go.

Good as New

Corey's mouth was so dry, it itched. He swallowed hard and tried to listen to Coach Phil.

"Great work, boys." Coach Phil congratulated them. "Only one more practice before the big game. See you tomorrow night."

Corey's mom was waiting on the sidelines. She smiled and handed him a water bottle as he came off the field. He took a deep long drink, but it didn't bring him any relief. His mouth tasted sour, and his stomach started cramping.

"What is it, Corey?" his mom looked at him in the rear view mirror on the way home. Corey's eyes were a little glassy, and he rarely sat so stiff and still.

"Nothing, I guess," Corey said slowly, thinking about the big game in two days. Then, more truthfully, he added, "I mean, I suppose my stomach hurts again."

Corey's mom frowned. He had been having stomachaches a little too frequently. Just last week she had taken Corey to see his doctor, but Dr. Jamison hadn't found anything serious. He had made a few suggestions; he hadn't even written a prescription.

"Maybe you're just a little over-tired," Mrs. Redmond said hopefully. Corey nodded. Tired–he certainly was that. Even though it was early, he was actually looking forward to going to bed.

Once home, Corey forced himself to shower and brush his teeth. Then he cautiously eased into his bed. If he lay perfectly still, his stomach might settle. He pulled up the covers and closed his eyes. He tried to pray, but he couldn't focus on more than a few short sentences. He was grateful that God heard small, weak prayers, as he fell into an uneasy sleep.

Corey dreamed he was riding his bicycle, taking a familiar route though the neighborhood. He was coming up on his favorite stretch of road—a long, gentle slope, perfect for a downward glide. He loved the cool breeze in his face and the whisk of his tires on the pavement as he coasted.

But this wasn't meant to be a peaceful ride. About halfway down the hill, Corey's tire struck a large rock. He felt himself hurtling forward, and his stomach slammed against the handlebars.

The pain jarred him awake, and Corey uncomfortably discovered that the pain wasn't a dream. He groaned. "Please, not the stomach flu!" But no amount of wishful thinking could keep the dreadful ache and nausea at bay. Corey was miserably sick.

His mom heard him run to the bathroom, and she met him as he returned to his room. She sat on the edge of his bed, gave him a hug, and stroked his forehead. "Corey, I think you have a fever. Let me get the thermometer."

"What is it, mom?" he whispered, after she took his temperature.

"It's a little high," she admitted. It was higher than she had expected. "It's one hundred and two."

Corey laid his head back on the pillow. He wanted to sleep, but his middle wouldn't let him. It was as if his insides held a bucket of pain and it was pouring out into his whole belly.

The following morning Corey felt a little bit better. He swatted at the alarm clock and tried to get up. If he didn't go to school, he couldn't practice soccer that evening and then he'd miss Saturday's game. But as he sat on the edge of the bed, he decided he just didn't care about missing practice.

His mom heard the alarm and came quickly to his room. "Good morning, Corey. Don't tell me you were thinking about going to school! You

were sick all night. You should stay home today, even if you do feel better. Do you feel better?"

"Not really."

"Oh, honey, I'm sorry. Tell me what hurts."

"I don't feel like throwing up, but my stomach really aches."

"Hmmm ... let me take your temperature again." He obediently held the thermometer in his mouth. "Down a little, but not much. I think I'll call Dr. Jamison again."

Corey sighed and lay back down on his bed. A few moments later his mom appeared and pulled out some clothes from his dresser.

"Sweetie, get up," she said, "Dr. Jamison says he will be in the office in a half an hour, and he wants us to come right in."

Corey was surprised. Was he really that sick? He had just been hoping that if he lay there long enough, he'd feel better. Besides, it would be nice if he could go back to sleep...

"Corey, I'm sorry. Please get up and get dressed. Don't you feel like eating anything? Even a cup of ice?"

Corey didn't feel like eating at all but agreed to take a cup of ice with him on the way to the doctor's office. However, the dull ache in his tummy certainly made food seem uninviting.

The nurse welcomed them as they came into the office.

"Thanks very much for seeing us so early," said Mrs. Redmond.

"Oh, you're welcome. Corey can sit here." She pointed to a table against the wall. Quickly she took his temperature and blood pressure. "Dr. Jamison will be right in. I hope you feel better soon." She smiled and exited.

The nurse had barely left, when Dr. Jamison entered the room. The doctor was a pleasant, bearded man with kind eyes and a brightly colored tie shining from under his white coat. He sympathetically surveyed the droopy little boy and patted Corey's mussed up hair.

"Not feeling too well today, Corey?"

"Not really."

"Ok, then, let's see what's up. Show me where it hurts. I'll be really careful and try not to poke you too hard," he added with a smile.

Corey was brave for the exam. He was too tired to complain much, anyway, but at one point he did go white, sitting bolt upright.

"Ouch!"

Dr. Jamison turned thoughtfully to Mrs. Redmond. "You know, Mrs. Redmond, I think

Corey may have appendicitis."

"Appendicitis?" Mrs. Redmond's eyes widened, although her voice stayed calm.

"Actually, yes... We'll take some blood work here, but I'd like you to see a surgeon. There's a good one in the building; his name is Dr. Sanderson. Why don't you take Corey on over? We'll call his office and tell them you're coming and give them our results."

"Alright, then, just tell me where to go," Mrs. Redmond responded.

Before Corey knew it, he was in another doctor's office. He leaned against his mom's shoulder and closed his eyes. He felt less sleepy than he had, and some questions were stirring in his head.

The office's interior door opened, and a

gentleman with bright red hair called his name. "Corey Redmond?" The man peered into the waiting room. "Please come with me," he added as he saw Corey and his mom rise. He ushered them into a small, clean-smelling room.

Again Corey's temperature and blood pressure were taken, and the man helped Corey climb onto the examination table. "Dr. Sanderson will be with you in just a few minutes."

Corey was now more awake than he had been all day. "Mom," he asked, "am I really sick? I feel better than I did last night. What's appendicitis?"

"Corey, I am glad you feel better; I've been praying for you all morning, and I'm really not sure how sick you are. You know, I think I hear the doctor coming. He's going to be able to answer both your and my questions."

Corey had been starting to feel nervous, and he was glad he hadn't had to wait very long for the doctor to come.

Dr. Sanderson was a tall, thin man with thinning dark hair and small, wire-rimmed glasses. His brown eyes were friendly, and his voice was encouraging when he greeted them. Corey felt a little calmer.

"It's nice to meet you, Corey and Mrs. Redmond." He shook Corey's mom's hand. "We've been in contact with Dr. Jamison, and he believes that Corey here might be troubled by appendicitis."

"Actually, yes," said Mrs. Redmond. "We hope you can tell us what is wrong."

"I think we should know that soon. First, I will do an examination. We should have the results of Corey's blood test soon, and that will help our diagnosis," Dr. Sanderson replied.

Corey held back the tears as the doctor checked his abdomen. The doctor saw his wincing, particularly when he pressed on Corey's lower right side. "Where does it hurt the most?" he asked.

"I guess mostly there!" Corey replied. "Although it hurts everywhere else too. Can you stop now?"

"Yes, I can. I'm sorry that hurt you, Corey."

"It's OK," Corey sighed.

"Mrs. Redmond, I do think that Dr. Jamison is correct. It does appear that Corey has appendicitis. I'm going to see about his blood work now. In the meantime, I'm going to ask you to go with my assistant, Mr. Morrison, to wait in my office."

Immediately, it seemed, the red-haired Mr. Morrison had appeared at the door. Corey and Mrs. Redmond were led into a quiet, plainly decorated office with a desk and several comfortable chairs. Corey was surprised to see his father sitting in one of the chairs.

"Hi, Dad!"

"Hey, sport! Hi, dear!" (He greeted Corey's mother.) "Come on over here, son, and sit next to your pop. How are you feeling?"

"I feel better. Just my stomach is sore. But I

haven't thrown up since last night!"

"Good." His dad hugged him.

A thought dawned on Corey, "Ummm .... Dad, why are you here?"

"Well, your mom called, and I thought I'd like to be here to see what's going on with my boy."

"Oh, OK, so what is going on?"

"I don't know yet, Corey."

"Oh."

A nurse appeared at the door. "Dr. Sanderson will be with you in about ten minutes. Thanks for waiting." She closed the door and left them in the quiet room.

Too quiet. Corey could feel his nervousness in his stomach, and it wasn't pleasant.

"Mom, I think I'm afraid."

"Sweetheart, I can understand that. It can be a fearful thing to be sick."

Corey's dad surprised them both by saying, "Dear, why don't you pray?" Corey wasn't sure he had heard him ask that before.

"Certainly," said Mrs. Redmond. She bowed her head and thanked the Lord that He was with them everywhere, including in the doctor's office. She asked the Heavenly Father to bless Corey and to give Dr. Sanderson wisdom to know how to help Corey. She prayed that the Savior would comfort Corey and ease his fears. At this Corey peeked and saw his dad wipe his eyes. But when the prayer was over, Mr. Redmond's voice was strong.

"Corey, when I was a boy, my mom used to quote a psalm when she was anxious. Something about the Lord being a shepherd. I thought I heard you reciting it the other day. Did you learn it for Sunday school?"

"Yes, Dad. It's Psalm 23."

"It used to comfort my mother when she would say it. Maybe it would help you too. Do you remember it?"

"Sure, Dad." Corey recited it perfectly from memory. It was one of his favorite psalms too. It was about how God looks after His people and protects them just like a shepherd looks after the sheep. It pleased Corey to hear that his Grandmother Redmond had known this Psalm. Dr. Sanderson opened the door at "surely goodness and mercy." He looked at them thoughtfully as Corey finished the verses. Then he entered quietly and sat down at the desk facing the Redmonds.

"We have all our results back, Mr. and Mrs. Redmond. Corey does have appendicitis."

"What is that?" the question burst out of Corey.

"Well, Corey, let me try to explain it simply." He showed Corey a picture he had on the desk.

"This is an appendix. It's like a little tube attached to your intestine. Sometimes it can get infected and make you really sick."

Corey headed straight for the bottom line. "How does it get better?" He tried to think of the worst scenario. "Do I have to get a shot?"

Dr. Sanderson cleared his throat, and Corey saw the adults glance at each other.

"Well, actually, Corey, that's not the way we help you recover from appendicitis. Another thing we do know about the appendix is that people live very normally without it, so when a person's

appendix is infected, the best way to treat it is to remove it."

Corey's eyes widened. He looked at the picture, at his stomach, and then back at Dr. Sanderson.

"Remove it? You mean take it out? How do you get it out of there? Does it hurt?" He was starting to feel a little dizzy.

His mom put her arm around him. "It's alright, Corey."

Dr. Sanderson smiled comfortingly. "Everything will be just fine, Corey. Let me tell you what will happen. First, your parents will take you over to the hospital." The hospital! Corey frowned nervously. Hospitals were for really, really sick people or maybe for having babies. He had hardly ever been in one.

Dr. Sanderson was still talking. "You'll go to a room with a bed, and some people will come and talk with you and your parents before the operation."

"But how do you get it out?" Corey was interrupting, but Dr. Sanderson didn't seem bothered at all.

"Well, that's the part I'm coming to, Corey. Another doctor will come and give you some medicine to help you go to sleep. We'll make a small incision—a small cut—and then we'll be able to take the appendix out. You won't feel anything at all because you'll be very sound asleep. It may hurt a little when you wake up, but we can give you some medicine for that too. You're a strong boy and otherwise in very good health, so you should recover quickly."

"I have a soccer game tomorrow."

"I'm sorry, Corey," Dr. Sanderson replied, "but you won't be able to play soccer for a few weeks."

"A few weeks? But the season will be over."

"You'll be able to play again next season, Corey. Your body will just need a little time to heal, but believe me, you'll feel as good as new in no time."

Corey grimaced. He wasn't sure he was too keen on this cutting-his-stomach stuff. Still, an operation! None of the kids he knew had ever had one. He pictured his friends visiting him in the hospital. "So, can we do this thing on Monday, maybe? I'd at least like to watch the game."

Dr. Sanderson tapped his pencil on the desk and looked at Corey compassionately. "Corey, since we know that you do have appendicitis, it would be unwise for us to wait. It will only get worse, and waiting might be dangerous. Tell me, Corey, have you had anything to eat or drink today?"

Corey remembered the ice chips, surely melted by now, still in the car's cup holder. "No, I didn't feel like it."

"Not even a drink of water?"

"No, sir. I didn't eat supper last night either."

"Good." Dr. Sanderson looked at Mr. and Mrs. Redmond. "I would like for you to take Corey over to the hospital just down the block. That's where I do my surgeries. We'll schedule an operating room, and we should be able to do the surgery by 5 PM today."

Corey looked at his mom. He was going to the

hospital! He didn't know whether to feel excited or scared. What would his friends think when he didn't show up for practice? "Mom, will you call Coach Phil?"

"Sure, honey."

Corey's nervousness seemed to make the next few hours fly by and yet drag at the same time. It was an odd feeling --- butterflies in his already sore stomach. Kind strangers were talking to him and his folks. He was wearing a funny hospital gown. He felt as if the operation time would never come, and that it was coming too quickly! Soccer practice seemed like a faint memory, like a bedtime story or a movie he hadn't seen in a while.

Pastor Freeling was Corey's first visitor. It made Corey feel happy to know that his friends knew what was happening and that they cared about him. Pastor Freeling read John 14:1–6 to his family. When he prayed with them, Corey felt like he could almost see the angels in the room with him, and he knew that Jesus would be with him in the operating room.

Finally, several green-robed adults were standing around his bed. As Corey looked away, one gentle lady put a needle into his arm. He was brave, even though he didn't like that feeling. When he looked back, there was a tube attached to his arm, and a bag was at the end of it. Medicine was dripping down the tube, and Corey had a cold sensation in his arm. But it didn't hurt too much, he decided.

"Corey," a man said, "we're going to put a

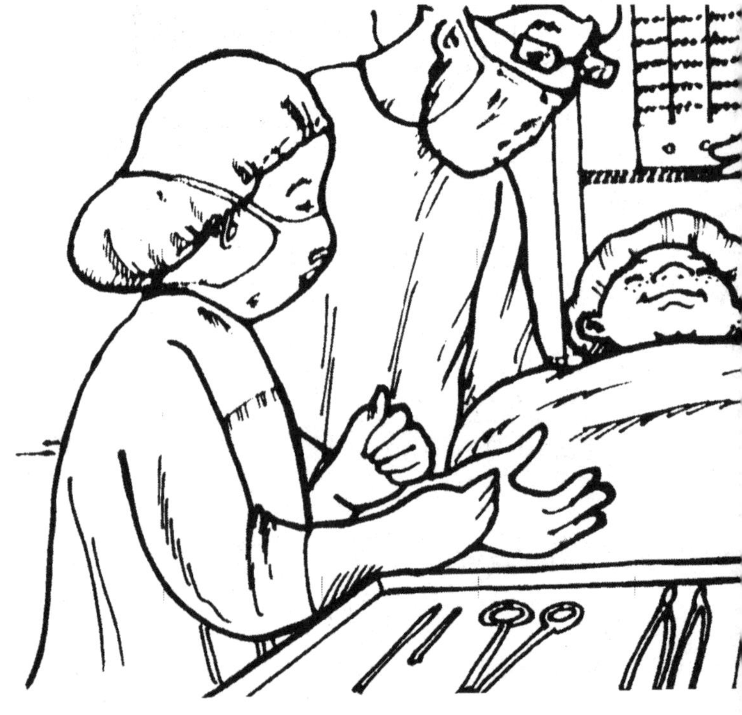

mask on your nose too, and we want you to breathe normally. These medicines will help you to go to sleep." He made some adjustments on a machine next to Corey. Corey wasn't sure he was ready, and he was beginning to feel a little light-headed.

"Count backwards from one hundred, Corey."

Corey's voice sounded funny to himself. "One hundred, ninety-nine, ninety-eight..."

Corey could hear some quiet music. It was very dark. He tried to open his eyes, but he couldn't manage it. It was really very dark… He thought he heard some voices too, but he was just so sleepy…

Corey knew there was some movement around him. He heard the voices again and recognized his mom's. He stirred, and then he felt her warm hand on his. He wanted to talk to her, but his lips were dry; and he still was having trouble opening his eyes.

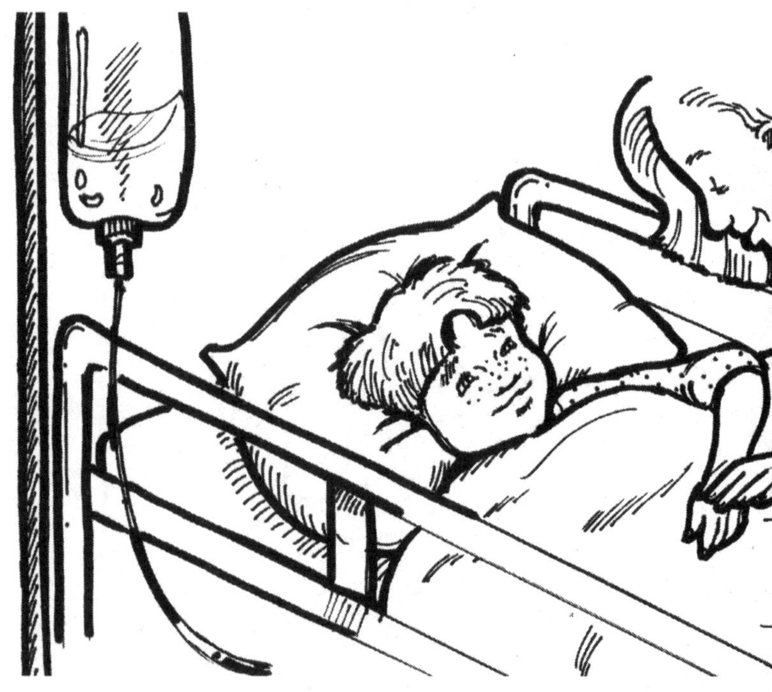

"Hi, sweetie, all done. Everything is just fine."

All done? Already? He sighed with relief and managed to open his eyes a slit, just enough to see his mom and her smile.

"Keep resting, Corey. Everything's fine."

Corey could hear his mom praying for him as he relaxed. He didn't try to open his eyes again...

When Corey finally woke up, he was a little sore. He still had a tube in his arm, and his head felt cloudy. He saw his mom and dad sitting in the

corner of the hospital room. It looked as if they were praying, but he wasn't sure. He lay quietly, trying not to disturb them. There was a Bible lying open on his dad's lap. Corey felt a warm, contented feeling coming over him.

Several weeks later, Corey and his dad were watching the Panthers win their last game of the season. Sitting next to Mr. Redmond was his now-close friend–Pastor Freeling. Corey grinned as he saw them talking together. Dr. Sanderson had been right. At that moment, Corey did feel as good as new.

ASK ABOUT IT

What was wrong with Corey?

Have you ever been very sick?

How did Corey feel about having to have an operation?

What verses did Corey's dad ask Corey to recite?

Have you memorized Psalm 23?

LESSON SPOT

Corey had to face a serious illness. Sometimes even children do become very ill. God uses sicknesses to teach His people many lessons. God used Corey's illness to help Corey learn to trust Him more. God also used the situation to cause Corey's dad to cry out to Him. Mr. Redmond saw that God was the One who was needed to help and comfort their family. When we are in trouble, we are not able to see or understand all of God's wise plan for us. Those are the times when we must ask Him to help us believe the promises He makes to His children. Memorizing God's word will help us face difficult times.

ASK YOURSELF

If you feel really disappointed about something what is the best thing to do? Pick your answers.

1. Go to your room and just feel miserable.

2. Get angry because it should never have happened to you.

3. Complain to your parents because they should have sorted it out.

4. Tell someone how you are disappointed and ask them to pray with you.

5. Thank God for all the good things that have happened to you.

6. Do something to help someone else. You might realise how well off you are then.

BIBLE VERSE

Isaiah 12:4

In that day you will say: "Give thanks to the LORD, call on his name; make known among the nations what he has done, and proclaim that his name is exalted.

Anna Banana
by Nancy Gorrell

Anna is absolutely, terribly, very annoyed with Corey Redmond! Pesky boy. Corey calls her Anna Banana and Anna does not like it one teeny-weeny bit! Corey even snatches Rose from Anna's loving arms and throws the doll in the air and whacks her on the floor. Pesky, pesky boy! There is no way that Anna is going to invite HIM to her birthday party! But Anna has to learn a lesson about forgiveness.

Become friends with Corey and Anna as they become friends with one another and with God.

Other Anna stories included in this book:
Fright in the Night: Anna learns a lesson about Trust
Cool Jewel: Anna learns a lesson about Gratitude.
ISBN: 9781845501822

Beginning with God by Nancy Gorrell

Nancy Gorrell wanted to find the right books to introduce her children to the truths of the faith. So she took up the challenge by writing for her own children. The first title, *Beginning with God*, covers God, the Bible, and the Trinity.

Nancy brings a contagious delight to these topics as she distils the great truths of God's Word. Discussing God, she answers such questions as "What does God look like?" "Will God always be here?" "Is God perfect?" and "Is God always fair?"

Nancy has also written *Meeting with God*, which covers the topics of creation, Jesus, and salvation and *Living with God*, which covers worship, heaven, obedience, and prayer. These books will be valuable resources for families and churches for years to come.

Beginning with God
ISBN: 9781857924534
Meeting with God
ISBN: 9781857925319
Living with God
ISBN: 9781857925326

CHRISTIAN FOCUS PUBLICATIONS
Christian Focus
Christian Heritage
CF4K
Mentor

CF4•K
Because you're never
to young to know Jesus